Franklin Rides a Bike

Franklin is a trade mark of Kids Can Press Ltd.

ISBN 0-439-04078-7

12 11 10 9 8 7 6   0 1 2 3 4/0

Printed in the U.S.A.   23

First Scholastic Club printing, May 1999

Franklin Rides a Bike

Paulette Bourgeois
Brenda Clark

SCHOLASTIC INC.
New York   Toronto   London   Auckland   Sydney

FRANKLIN could swim underwater and hit a home run. He knew how to climb the monkey bars and pump himself high on the swings. But Franklin had a problem. He couldn't ride his bicycle without training wheels.

In the spring, all of Franklin's friends had training wheels on their bikes.

Beaver was the brave one. She took her extra wheels off first.

She practiced and practiced. Then she went to the park to show off.

"Look at me!" she shouted. "I can ride my bike all by myself."

Franklin watched Beaver ride around in circles.

It wasn't long before Beaver could signal with one paw and hold on to the handlebar with the other.

Soon, everyone but Franklin could ride without training wheels.

"We're going on a picnic," said Bear. "Come on."

Franklin was worried that his friends would make fun of his training wheels.

"I'm not hungry," Franklin fibbed. He went home to eat lunch, alone.

Afterwards, Franklin asked his mother to help take the training wheels off his bike. He wanted to ride all by himself.

He sat on his bike, and his mother gave him a push.

Franklin wibbled and wobbled, and teetered and tottered. Then he fell into the flower bed.

"I can't do it," he said. "I'm never riding this bike again."

For the rest of the week, Franklin felt left out.
He watched as his friends rode off without him.
They were becoming great explorers on their bikes.

On Saturday, Franklin's friends zoomed by his house.

"That looks like fun," said Franklin's mother.

"I can't ride without my training wheels," groaned Franklin.

"Did you give it your best effort?" asked his
mother.

"Well ..." said Franklin. "Maybe I could try
one more time."

Franklin sat on his bike.

"It's tippy!" he cried.

His mother held on to the seat. "Try it. I won't let go until you tell me to."

Franklin pedaled while his mother guided the bicycle from behind.

He felt unsteady and very unsure.

"I'm going to fall," he said, and he stopped pedaling.

"Riding a bicycle is difficult," said his mother.
"But you can't give up just because it's frustrating."

"It's too hard for me," said Franklin. "It was easy
for my friends."

"Do you think *everything* comes easily for them?"
she asked.

Franklin had to think about that.

Franklin went to the park.

He saw Beaver struggling to swing on the monkey bars. Each time she got to the third rung, she fell into the sand below.

"No, Beaver," said Bear. "Do it like this. It's easy."

"Easy for you," said Beaver.

She tried one more time and fell again.

"Maybe tomorrow," Beaver grumbled.

Franklin remembered when Badger learned to swim. She was afraid to put her head underwater.

"It's easy," said Franklin. "Just do it!"

Badger had spluttered and cried. It took her a long time to feel good in the water. Now she could swim from one end of the pond to the other.

Franklin thought about the first time Fox played baseball.

He couldn't hit the ball at all. But he tried and tried until, one day, Fox got a home run.

Just then, Porcupine came by.

She moved *very* slowly. She pointed to the pads on her knees, wrists and elbows.

"They make me feel funny," she said, "but they keep me safe."

"That's it!" cried Franklin. He hurried home.

Franklin put on padding. He lined the walk with old pillows.

"I'm ready to try again," Franklin told his mother. "Now I won't worry if I fall."

Franklin sat on his bike, and his mother held on to the seat.

Franklin wibbled and wobbled, and teetered and tottered.

He fell many times but he never gave up.

Then it happened. Franklin told his mother
to let go. He didn't veer into the bushes, and he
didn't crash.

"Way to go!" cheered his mother.

Franklin was thrilled. Finally, he was riding
his bike all by himself.

"I can do it!" he shouted.

Franklin rode to the park to show his friends.

"Look at me!" he called.

Franklin tried to signal with one hand, like Beaver, but he toppled over.

"I think I'll work on that," he laughed. "Not everything is as easy as it looks."